Dear Caitlin

For someone who shares a gre[at]
love for our cats!

Best,

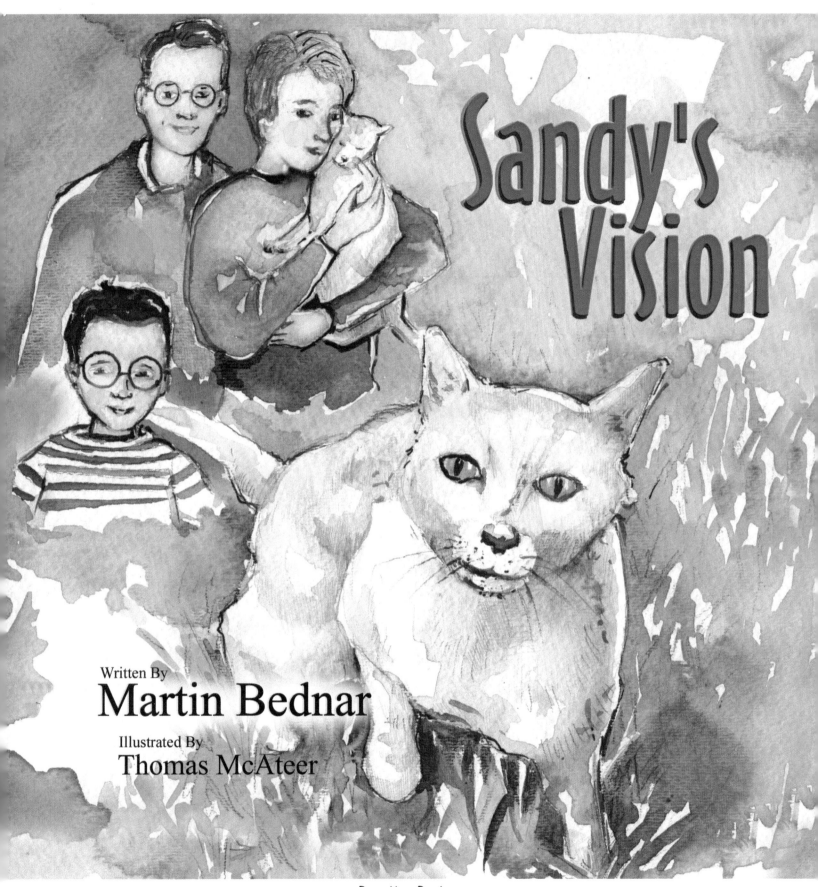

Sandy's Vision

Written By
Martin Bednar

Illustrated By
Thomas McAteer

Bear Hug Books
An Imprint of MidAmerica Publishing Company
Georgetown, Texas
www.mpcbooks.com

Bear Hug Books, An Imprint of MidAmerica Publishing Company,
40120 Industrial Park Circle
Suite C
Georgetown, Texas 78626
1-800-283-4142
Visit us on the web at www.mapubco.com; or see our books at www.mpcbooks.com.

The illustrations for this book were rendered on paper and digitally remastered for publication. This book is printed and manufactured
in the United States of America.

❖❖❖❖❖❖❖❖❖❖❖❖❖❖❖❖❖❖❖❖❖❖❖❖❖❖❖

10 9 8 7 6 5 4 3 2 1   v First Edition, Hardcover

ISBN 13: 978-1-933732-15-2
ISBN 10: 1-933732-15-6

Library of Congress Control Number 2006909556
CIP data for this book can be found at the Library of Congress.

❖❖❖❖❖❖❖❖❖❖❖❖❖❖❖❖❖❖❖❖❖❖❖❖❖❖❖

This book is dedicated to:

My nieces and nephews: Jonathan, Elizabeth, Justin, Jordan, Marty, Randy, Lisa, Timmy, Peter and Thomas, JJ, Tyler and Tory, Brendan, Kylie and Clarkie. Your innate enthusiasm, optimism, and the profound insight of childhood affords me with endless opportunities to grow and learn.

My parents and my entire family. Your unwavering and unconditional love and support provides the framework for my life and genuine meaning for my achievements.

Most especially to my wife, Arlean. With your guidance and by your example, you have provided me with the courage and fortitude to pursue my dreams, regardless of the challenge and irrespective of the outcome...and to also remember what is important along the way.

Please help us... help needy animals.

MidAmerica Publishing Company donates a portion of the proceeds from all sales to the Save My Shelter Fund. The fund was developed to help animal shelters, nationwide, deal with the overwhelming need to provide community education, animal rescue and care, and operate adoption programs that find needy animals loving homes. By buying our books, dogTaggs, or any of our publishing related products, you are helping too. The nation's needy animals, animal shelters in each of our local communities, and our company extend a gracious and hearty Thank You. Thank you very much.

For more information on the Save My Shelter™ Fund, please visit: www.savemyshelter.org.
For more information on our dogTaggs™ Product line, please visit: www.dogtaggs.com.

Scott C. Damschroder
Publisher
MidAmerica Publishing Company

Running down the hill toward the big pond to meet his summer friends, Clarkie could not think of anywhere else he would rather be.

This summer would be very special. Clarkie had been waiting all year to spend his vacation in the country with Aunt Arlean, Uncle Marty and their two kittens, Holly and Ivy.

Now at the edge of the pond, Clarkie watched and listened for all the greetings. Frogs sang by the cattails, Turtles napped in the sun and fish leaped high above the calm pond surface, hoping to catch a dragonfly for lunch.

One summer's day, as Holly and Ivy stretched out in the
sun on the old brick wall, they suddenly stood up, meowing
as loudly as they possibly could.
"What are those two little kittens up to now?"
wondered Aunt Arlean as she ran outside to see what all the
fuss was about.

Clarkie also heard the loud meows and ran up from
the pond. Soon they saw the reason for all the excitement.
There on the lawn was a very handsome cat. He was sitting
quietly in the grass, looking at Holly and Ivy as if to ask
what all the noise was about.

Clarkie and Aunt Arlean walked over to say 'hello' and
he greeted them with a 'Meow' and a swish of his long tail.
His thick fur was the color of the pond's sandy beach, so
Aunt Arlean named him Sandy Cat.

"Sandy is very friendly," said Clarkie, as the
purring cat rubbed against his leg.
"But he looks hungry and he is very thin.
Can we give him something to eat?"

Aunt Arlean smiled and soon Clarkie was helping to
prepare a saucer of milk and a bowl of cat treats.
Sandy quickly lapped up the milk, but he ran away after
trying to eat only one cat treat.

Clarkie did not understand why Sandy left so quickly,
so that night he had many questions for Uncle Marty
and Aunt Arlean.
"Why didn't Sandy Cat eat the cat treats like Holly and Ivy do?
Why is he so thin? Do you think he will visit us again?
Do you think Sandy has a home?"

"Well, I don't think Sandy has a home because he doesn't
have a collar or a name tag," said Aunt Arlean.
"Sandy is also very, very thin, so I don't think anyone else
is even feeding him."

Over the next week, Sandy Cat came to visit every day and
every day Clarkie was waiting to greet him. Clarkie carefully
watched as Sandy ate and would gently pet him after each
bite of food.

Meanwhile, Uncle Marty asked all the neighbors near and far
but no one was missing Sandy Cat.
"He is always here, this is Sandy's home," Clarkie said.
Uncle Marty and Aunt Arlean smiled and nodded in agreement.

"You have a new friend," Uncle Marty added,
as Clarkie gently picked up Sandy Cat.

Sandy loved to be held. When he sat on Clarkie's
lap, he could feel Sandy's rumbling purr all through
his body.

But Clarkie was worried about Sandy.
"He doesn't ever eat all his food," he said to Aunt Arlean.
"And I can hold him for a long time and he is not even heavy."

He thought for a moment.
"Maybe Sandy can't eat. Do you think we can take him to
the doctor and see if anything is wrong?" he asked.
"Yes" said Aunt Arlean. "That is a very good idea."

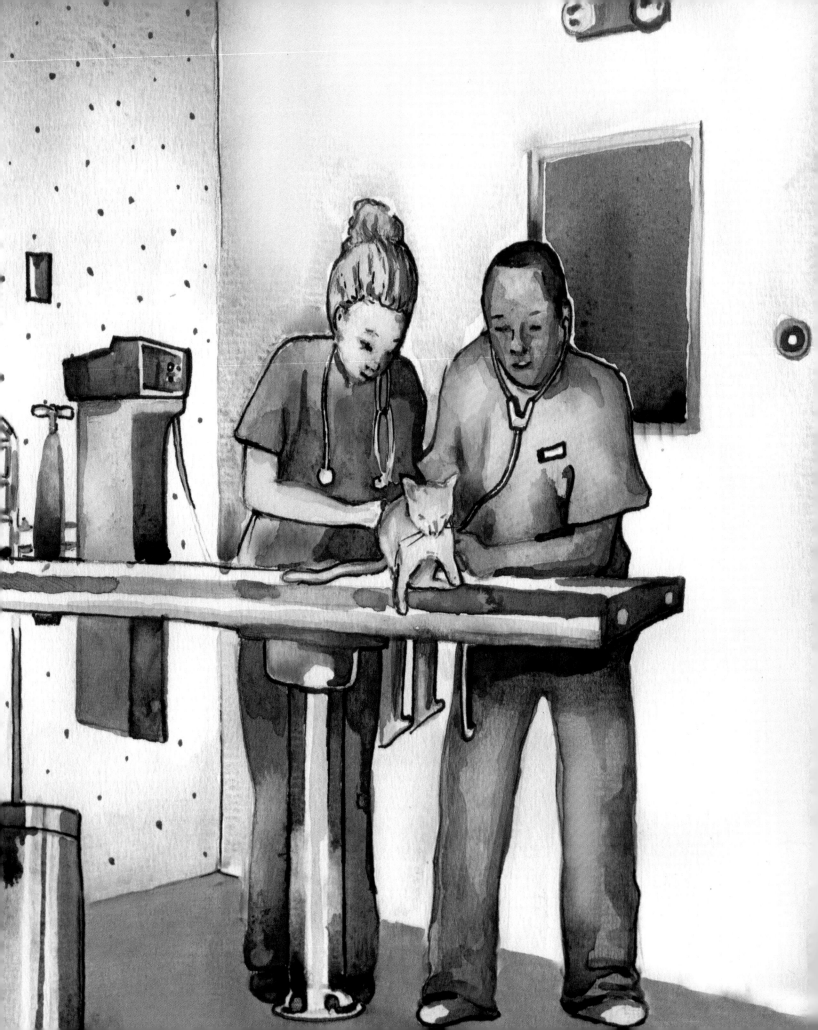

That next day, the doctor met Sandy Cat,
Clarkie and Aunt Arlean.

She gave Sandy a big hug and rubbed his neck.
He liked that very much, and Clarkie smiled.

The doctor felt Sandy's belly. She looked at his
eyes and then she looked into his mouth.

"Well," she said, "I can see why Sandy is so thin
and isn't eating. Sandy has had an infection of his
teeth and mouth for a very long time, and now it
hurts too much for him to eat. Only an operation
can help him, but it will be very difficult."

The room was suddenly very quiet.

Clarkie was holding Sandy Cat very close, as Aunt Arlean gently rubbed the back of his neck. The doctor looked at Aunt Arlean and Clarkie.

She knew that they cared about Sandy very much. Finally, Clarkie announced:
"We need to try to get Sandy well; I can help take care of him."
His eyes bright and his voice confident that the decision for surgery had now been made.

Aunt Arlean nodded in agreement and the doctor smiled. Sandy's eyes were closed and his paws dangled loosely, but the swishing of his tail told everyone that he knew he was loved.

That night, Aunt Arlean and Clarkie explained everything to Uncle Marty. The operation would be scheduled soon. They fed Sandy soft baby food. He was very hungry and ate it all, purring loudly between each spoonful.

After dinner, Sandy fell asleep in Clarkie's lap, his paw folded over Clarkie's arm.

The morning of the surgery arrived and the operation was very long indeed. Uncle Marty, Aunt Arlean and Clarkie waited anxiously for any news.

When the doctor called, Uncle Marty spoke to her for a long time. Uncle Marty looked very serious. As he hung up the phone, he was quiet for a moment. He then explained to Aunt Arlean and Clarkie that the surgery was very, very difficult because the infection was much worse than the doctor had expected.

She told Uncle Marty that Sandy's mouth would get better and that he would be able to eat. But the doctor also explained that the infection had caused other problems during the surgery and that right now Sandy does not seem to be able to walk or see because of this.

The doctor was going to stay with Sandy Cat all night long and would call in the morning to tell us how he is doing.
At first, Clarkie sat quietly. Holly was curled up on his lap. He continued to look down and gently pet her as he thought about what Uncle Marty had told him. Aunt Arlean came over and placed her arms on Clarkie's shoulders. Both of them now had a tear running down their cheeks.

Finally, Clarkie raised his head. "I feel very sad," he said. Uncle Marty and Aunt Arlean nodded.
"What can we do?" Clarkie asked, sniffling a bit as he spoke.

"Well" said Uncle Marty, "We need to think about what is most important to us. Like showing how much we love each other and doing our best to help each other. This is what we can do right now."

And with that, Uncle Marty and Aunt Arlean gave
Clarkie a big hug and wiped the tear off his cheek.

Clarkie looked up and asked "Can we see Sandy
in the morning and show him how much we love him too?"
"Yes," said Uncle Marty. "I think this is exactly what
we should do."

Clarkie nodded and smiled a bit and they all began
to think about tomorrow's visit.

The next day at the animal hospital, they
found Sandy wrapped in a bright plaid blanket.
"He knows we're here," Clarkie smiled, as
Sandy's ears stood straight up and his tail
swished from side to side.

They gently rubbed Sandy behind his ears and
fed him lunch. When he weakly meowed, Clarkie
knew that Sandy was saying that he really wanted
to come home. But he had to stay in the hospital
for a week. Clarkie visited Sandy every day.

At last the doctor said, "Sandy is ready to go home,
but he will need a lot of help and attention."
With a nod and a big smile, Clarkie helped the
doctor wrap Sandy Cat in his bright plaid blanket.
Only his head and his swishing tail were visible.

As Aunt Arlean and Clarkie walked in to the house,
Holly and Ivy welcomed Sandy with loud 'Meows.'
But while they played with bird feathers, furry toy
mice, and bright balls, Sandy Cat did not play at all.
Sandy could not walk or see.

Clarkie knew that Sandy most definitely could hear
and smell.
"When I say hello, Sandy's ears get taller. And look
how he can find his cat treats," said Clarkie, as Sandy
sniffed from one side to the other until he found them.
"He can even eat his treats now, and he feels heavier
when I pick him up. He is gaining weight!" exclaimed Clarkie.

Over the next few weeks, Sandy slowly learned how to
crawl. Clarkie would hold Sandy up as he tried to walk.
He was very patient and would gently whisper to Sandy
to encourage him. But Clarkie sometimes wondered if
Sandy would ever walk again. No one knew.

Clarkie would quietly pet Sandy from his head to his tail
as he thought about his friend. Aunt Arlean and Uncle
Marty watched and smiled as Clarkie and Sandy learned
from each other.
"Don't give up," they told him, and Clarkie and Sandy
would try again.

And then one day, Sandy slowly walked over to Clarkie
and rubbed against his leg. A swish of his tail said,
"I am getting better!" Clarkie picked Sandy Cat up and
gave him a big hug. And it was in that moment that they
both learned a great lesson about doing something that's
really important, even when it's not very easy.

Uncle Marty and Aunt Arlean were very, very proud.

Clarkie thought for a moment and said, "Uncle Marty, do you think Sandy is ready for more company?"
"Yes," said Uncle Marty, "maybe when your mom and dad come to visit, we can also invite all your cousins to see Sandy Cat too."

Clarkie's big smile said that this was exactly what he was hoping for.

On a crisp, cool late summer day, Clarkie's cousins all came. Holly and Ivy stretched out on the wooden beams high above the living room, looking down on all the excitement. Clarkie's cousins brought out the furry toy mice, bird feathers, and bright balls. They were puzzled when Sandy did not play with any of the cat toys. Soon, all of the cousins lost interest.

As they began to walk away, Clarkie could hear them say "This cat's no fun, he can't see anything." Someone added, "What good is a blind cat anyway?"

Clarkie went over and picked up Sandy, holding him close.
Sandy Cat knew he was loved and he liked this the most.

"Sandy can see", said Clarkie, in a most definite tone,
as he looked over at Aunt Arlean and Uncle Marty.
The room grew quiet.

"Sandy sees a lot!" he repeated. Clarkie's cousins were now
even more curious than ever.

Clarkie explained. "Sandy Cat sees how much we love him
and how much we love each other. This love helps us even
when we are sad or when we are scared, and it makes us feel
even better when we are happy. It also helps us not to give
up when we have something to do that's not very easy.
Isn't that right, Uncle Marty?"

With a tear in his eye, a gigantic hug, and an equally huge smile, Uncle Marty answered. "Yes, Clarkie. This is the love that you share with your parents and cousins today and that you have shared with us and Sandy Cat all summer long."

And cuddled gently in Clarkie's arms, the swishing of Sandy Cat's soft, long tail showed that he very much agreed!

MEOW!!!